Dedicated to:

Brad Bates for making my crazy ideas come to life.

Lauren Colvin for painting my LFL.

And to all the kids and families that have visited my LFL.

The Traveling Book

Can you find a kitty on each page?

Written by
Charissa Bates

Illustrated by
Nadja Bullis

Hey there! Yes, this is your book talking to you! You look like a new friend. Let me introduce myself....I'm the traveling book!

Let me tell you a little bit about my travels! Right after I was printed, I was shipped off to a bright new store. There I sat next to the most beautiful books I've ever seen. It was so exciting! **"Hello, cashier! Hello, books! Hello, kitty!"** I greeted everyone.

The next day, a lady walked over and picked up a few books. **"Pick me! Pick me!"** I squealed. To my excitement, she paged through me and looked at all of my colorful pictures.

"Now wait! Not too tight!"

Into the cart I went and before I knew it, she was wrapping some glittery paper all around me.

Suddenly it was dark...

Light! There was light and someone was looking at me! She looked very nice.

...I heard giggles all around.

One of my favorite days was when they read me in front of an entire classroom of kids.

Reading time

"They love me!"

My friend asked her dad to read me several times at bedtime.

"Goodnight, friend!"
I whispered.

Then she put me on her nightstand. I was on this nightstand for a whole week.
"Hello? Friend? Can you read me...pretty please?"
I was getting worried...

Later I got moved to the bookshelf. My friend still picked me up to read from time to time but not very often.

Then one day her mom started grabbing books and putting them in boxes! This was very strange to me. She opened me up, read through a few pages, and then placed me in a box. A big red book fell on me.

"Ouch! Excuse me!!"

Into the castle looking structure I went between two board books! It said "Little Free Library" on the front!

Free Little Library

MN

The next day a family showed up.
They put a few books in and pulled me
out. Once home, the boy opened me up
and read me right away!

"New friends!!"

Little Free Library

From there I went to other Little Free Libraries.

I was at a library that had books with bumps for words. These help kids who cannot see to read. (I discovered it was called Braille)

Check out this one built like a barn.

One day I got packed into a suitcase and up, up, up I went in the sky. I landed in Norway, in a little town called Voss. They read me on a picnic and served a delicious dessert called Lefse.

I went on a shelf for a few years after that. Can you believe that - years! No one ever noticed me. **"How rude!"** Finally I ended up in their Little Free Library.

Countryside Lefse
4,854 miles →

Often I'm a little sad when my reader is done with me, but I was really enjoying the mountains and streams in Norway.

Later I lived with a large family for awhile. They read me a lot. It was a busy house full of love. Cousins would come over for story time - it was fun to be read with so many people surrounding me. Then off to a box I went again.

And just when I thought no one would ever read me again, I was brought home by these nice grandparents. I got to snuggle up on the lap of this boy while grandma read me.

"Snuggles! It's been so long!"

I heard "lights out" and there was stillness. Then this bright light shined on me. I didn't mind, because two little hands were holding me tight. He quietly read me.

"This kitty's paw is tickling me! Heehee!"

"I love sharing my story when people read me. I am happy when I make new friends through my travels. "

"...and all my travels have led me to you.

How lucky am I?!"

PLACES I'VE BEEN

Where did you get me?

NC

WI

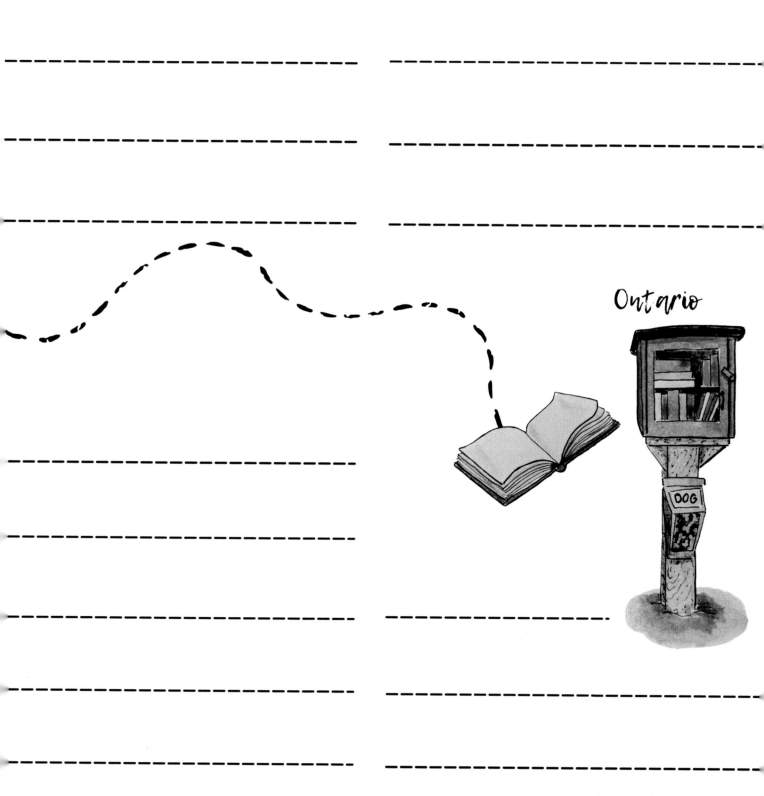

Ontario

Things Charissa Likes

Little Free Libraries

Coffee

Cats

Being a Survivor

Campir

Charissa is a mother to three beautiful children. She is a survivor of a rare and aggressive cancer. She works as a Children's Mental Health Therapist and enjoys serving and volunteering. Charissa loves her Little Free Library that looks like a castle. She enjoys creating, bringing her children on adventures, camping, and traveling. During cancer Charissa discovered how therapeutic writing was for her. Thus, three books were born: We Find Joy: Cancer Messed with the Wrong Family ,The Traveling Book and Meet the Wildflowers. She lives by the words "Find Joy". Again, her most important role is being able to watch her three beautiful children grow up.

Nadja has always loved stories, coming from a family of readers. Her grandfather would often tell her stories and her grandmother taught her how to draw.

Now she likes to tell stories with her art, like this one! After suffering a concussion, she had to stay home for a year and during that time started to focus on her art business with help of her loving family. She looks to use her work to advocate for mental health. You can find her work at www.nadjastudio.com

Cats

Things Nadja Likes

Tea

Making cute things

Fairytales

Made in the USA
Columbia, SC
05 August 2022

64697577R00020